The Pawn's Puzzlement

Valerie Munro

The Pawn's Puzzlement

BOOK ONE OF

'THE CHECKMATES'

SERIES

VALERIE MUNRO

This is a work of fiction. All of the characters, organizations, and events portrayed in this novel are either products of the author's imagination or are used fictitiously.

THE PAWN'S PUZZLEMENT

First Edition: December 2022

Produced in the United States of America

0 9 8 7 6 5 4 3 2 1

Acknowledgements

The pieces on the chess board are stronger when backed up by other pieces, and the same holds true in the writing and publication of *The Pawn's Puzzlement*. Wil Mara, there are not enough words in the English language to express how indebted I am to you for your brilliance with editing, cover design, and prowess in chess, but most of all for believing in this story and helping my dream become a reality. Thank you to my friends, Tom Andrea, and Elisabeth Schmitt, for reading an early manuscript and lending your expertise with details. A heap of gratitude goes out to the students at Hillview School who have played chess in the library during recess throughout the years- you have inspired this story! Thank you, Imad Khachan, owner of Chess Forum in Greenwich Village, NYC. You are one of the kindest, most open-hearted human beings I have ever met. I will never forget the day you gave me chess books and sets for my students, and I cannot wait to bring you copies of this book to give away to young players. Deb Kusiak, I treasure your friendship and love of the game and you will always be my favorite opponent! Finally, I am so blessed to have the encouragement of my loving family. Edward, thank you for the stories about your grandparents' farm and for sharing every moment of this exciting adventure with me. Nicholas and Victoria, thank you for your support and I hope you will use your social media connections to ensure that millions of folks read this book. Whether you have been part of the opening, middlegame or endgame, this book would not have possible without all of you.

THE CHESS PIECES IN THIS STORY

WHITE PIECES

The Royals
King Edward

Queen Nora

Rooks
Warwick Castle

Calvay Castle

Knights
Sir John

Dame Mary

Bishops
Bishop Channing

Bishop Kirby

Pawns
Piers

Peter

Phoebe

Peri

Phinian

Porter

Paul

Percipia

BLACK PIECES

The Royals
King George

Queen Beatrice

Rooks
Kenfig Castle

Stirling Castle

Knights
Sir Nicholas

Sir Charles

Bishops
Bishop Reginalt

Bishop Preston

Pawns
Parker

Penelope

Portia

Pippa

Prentice

Philip

Philbert

Prudence

For my daughter, Victoria

Chapter 1

IT WAS just after two thirty in the afternoon, and Gram and Pop's barn sale was coming to an end. Three long wooden tables had been jam-packed with all sorts of old stuff earlier in the morning, but now only a handful of items remained: a stack of brown dishes, some old records, and a pair of polka dot gardening gloves.

Gram rose from her plastic lawn chair and picked up the gloves.

"I'm surprised nobody bought these," she remarked wistfully. "They're barely used."

"Well, you won't need them at Shady Acres," Pop pointed out. "The groundskeepers take care of the gardens. It's included with the rent."

Garrett couldn't believe Gram and Pop were moving to a retirement village. For as long as he could remember, they had lived in this large white farmhouse with the wraparound porch.

The gray barn in the back field was home to an old pasture horse named Josh, but just this morning, he had been led away on his halter by a young girl in long braids named Kimmy. Horses were not allowed at Shady Acres. Thinking back on this morning's scene and Josh's empty stall also made Garrett feel sad.

"Won't you miss Josh? Won't you miss the farm?" The words tumbled out of Garrett's mouth as he stretched his arms wide and spun around. "Won't you miss *all of this*?"

Pop threw his head back and laughed. Then, seeing how upset Garrett was, he covered his mouth and coughed instead.

"*Of course* we'll miss Josh," he said. "And the farm, too. But with my bad back and Gram's arthritis, we just can't keep up with it anymore."

Garrett sighed. "It won't be the same."

"No, it's going to be even *better*," Gram reassured him. "Shady Acres has an indoor swimming pool, a bowling alley, and an ice cream parlor! You're going to love visiting us there!"

Garrett smiled weakly.

"Now, why don't you see if you can hunt down Max for us," Pop suggested. "The family that's adopting him should be here soon."

Even Max, the tabby cat, was leaving. He had been catching mice in the gray barn for years. But cats weren't allowed at Shady Acres, either.

"I think I saw him out back near the toolshed earlier," Gram said.

As Garrett headed out of the barn to search for Max, a young woman passed by. She was out of breath, as though she had run all the way there, and was waving a dollar bill in the air.

"Are the garden gloves still available? I came back for them!"

Garrett pretended as though he didn't see her and kept walking.

It was dark.

It had been pitch-black for a very long time.

There had been light once. But it was so long ago that Piers, the pawn, could barely remember it.

Maybe it had just been a dream.

Chapter 2

"MAX! MAX!" Garrett called.

Perhaps Max knows he has to leave the farm and is hiding, Garrett thought. He peered down each row of Pop's dying corn stalks, hoping to catch sight of the tabby. But all he saw were a few moths flitting among the tall, withering plants.

"If nobody catches him, maybe he'll just stay here," Garrett said out loud with a shrug. Then, recalling what Gram had mentioned about the toolshed, he set off in that direction.

The door of Pop's toolshed was slightly open, and Garrett stepped inside. He had always loved hanging around here, watching Pop build and fix things. He especially liked the stories that Pop told him while he worked.

But now even the toolshed was empty. Pop had placed an ad on eBay and sold all of his tools except one hammer, one screwdriver, and a box of nails.

There are people at Shady Acres who fix anything that breaks, Garrett remembered him saying.

There was still some sawdust on the floor, a reminder of Pop's many woodworking projects. Garrett recalled the time Pop helped him make a train whistle. Then Max suddenly brushed by his leg and darted off toward the back of the shed.

"Max, come over here!" cried Garrett. "Max!"

He took off after the cat, and the two dashed around in circles until Max finally scooted underneath Pop's workbench. Garrett got down on the dusty floor and peered underneath. Max was flattened against the back wall, his green eyes staring back.

"Now I've gotcha!" Garrett whispered triumphantly.

Something was going on out there.

Piers was sure of it.

He couldn't see what it was, but he could hear it.

The pawn felt something he hadn't felt in a long time.

Hope.

Chapter 3

GARRETT BEGAN crawling on his stomach toward Max. The cat eyed him warily, his tail twitching from side to side.

Gram is going to kill me, Garrett thought. *We're going out to dinner tonight, and now my clothes will be filthy. All because Max decided to hide under the workbench.*

Garrett extended his arm and continued moving forward. As soon as he got close enough, he began brushing his fingertips against Max's silky fur. Max started purring. This soon grew so loud that it sounded like a locomotive was traveling through the toolshed. Then Max closed his eyes. He was falling asleep.

"Now stay still," Garrett muttered. He shifted his arm until it was wrapped around the cat's middle. Then he pulled Max toward him.

Max responded to this by letting out a yowling shriek! His claws dug deep as he wriggled out of Garrett's grasp!

Once he was free, he headed toward the door.

Garrett sat up quickly to chase after him, but he banged his head hard against the underside of the workbench. His brain immediately felt fuzzy. He made one last grab at the cat's tail before everything went black, but Max was gone a second later, leaving Garrett passed out cold on the floor.

Sir Nicholas heard the commotion and awoke with a start.

"We are under siege!" he yelled.

"Huzzah!" cried the other knights— Sir John, Sir Charles, and Dame Mary. They had been waiting for this moment forever.

All the knights drew their swords with a flourish.

"God save the Kings!" they cried.

Chapter 4

GARRETT came around quickly, but it took him several moments to remember why he was lying underneath Pop's workbench. He recalled chasing Max there, but the creature was long gone now.

His arm smarted from where Max had scratched him, and an egg-shaped lump had swelled on the top of his head. He definitely needed an ice pack and some Band-Aids. He began sliding backwards, being careful to not to bump his head again. Then something caught his eye as he was about to stand up. A beam of sunlight slanting through the window had landed on *something* back in the corner under the workbench. There was a twinkle. A glint. He squinted and saw that that it was a wooden box of some sort. The light had caught one of the box's metal hinges.

Pop must have missed the box when he cleaned things out.

Thinking that Pop would probably want to sell whatever was in it, Garrett crawled forward, grabbed the box by the handle, and dragged it along the floor as he backed out. It was surprisingly light, and he heard a bunch of things rolling around inside of it.

He got up and carried the box outside so he could take a better look at it. It was certainly old. Using the tip of his index finger, he wrote his name in the layer of dust that covered it. Then he tried opening the latch, but it wouldn't pop. He shook the box and wondered what was inside. Well, he hadn't caught the cat, but he was sure Pop would be happy that he'd found this box.

He tucked it under his arm and headed back to the barn.

It was utter chaos. Absolute confusion.

Without warning, their box had been turned on its side and the pieces were tossed wildly about. They crashed into each other and slid in all directions.

"What's happening?" cried Queen Nora.

"It's an earthquake!" declared King Edward.

"Everyone, please remain calm," urged Bishop Reginalt.

But that was easier said than done. Because now the box began swaying from side to side.

"I believe we are on the high seas!" declared King George.

Chapter 5

"WHAT IN the world happened to you?" exclaimed Gram. She and Pop were still sitting in their lawn chairs. And—Garrett couldn't believe his eyes—Max was settled calmly on Gram's lap!

In the excitement of finding the wooden box, he had completely forgotten about how he looked. His dust-covered shirt. His bloody, scratched arm.

"I'm okay," he said, "but I hit my head on the workbench when I was chasing after Max." He shot a disgusted look at the cat. "I think I may have even knocked myself out for a bit."

"Heavens!" Gram rose quickly, forcing Max to the ground. The cat looked a little disgruntled and resettled himself under Pop's chair.

"Let me see," Gram went on. She felt about in Garrett's hair and looked troubled when her fingers found the large lump. "Sit here by Pop while I get some ice," she said, then took off toward the house.

Garrett flopped into Gram's chair with the box on his lap.

"What's that you have?" Pop asked.

"I found it under your workbench. Maybe there are more tools inside?"

Pop's brow furrowed. "I don't recall seeing that particular box before. It must have belonged to the farm's previous owners." Pop smiled. "Well, no matter. It's yours."

"But you don't even know what's in here," Garrett pointed out.

"Doesn't matter," Pop laughed. "Gram and I are getting rid of things, remember?"

"The latch is stuck," Garrett told him, handing the box over.

Pop tried the latch, but it didn't budge.

"I think this is a job for the All-In-One," Pop grinned. A few years ago, Garrett had given the All-In-One pocket tool to Pop for his birthday. It was actually seven tools in one: nail clipper, bottle opener, pliers, scissors, flathead screwdriver, ruler, and hammer. Pop had proclaimed that it was the best gift he'd ever received and looked for any opportunity to use it.

He wedged the screwdriver under the latch and pressed down. The latch popped open with a loud click. Then he and Garrett peered into the box together.

Pop let out a low whistle.

"Well, would you look at that!"

"Oh happy day!" cried Queen Beatrice. "Sunshine!"

"How we have dreamt of it! How we have longed for it!" smiled Queen Nora. She blinked in the bright light.

"The air! So much crisper than stale box air!" announced Warwick Castle. He flung open his windows to let the breeze in.

"Hey! Don't hog all of it!" snorted Stirling Castle as he heaved his heavy front door open.

"Don't be silly," admonished Bishop Channing. "There's plenty of air to go around."

Hearing that, all of the pieces closed their eyes and inhaled deeply.

"Ahhhhh," they all exhaled. Over and over they breathed in and breathed out.

It was Piers who first became aware of the two faces staring down at them.

"Giants!" he screamed. "Hurry! Shut the box!"

Chapter 6

"I CAN'T believe it!" Pop exclaimed. "To think, a chess set was hidden underneath my workbench all these years and I never knew it! And by the looks of it, someone whittled these pieces themselves. Maybe they were made right there in the toolshed."

Garrett picked up one of the smallest white pieces. He turned it over in his fingers, examining it.

"That's a pawn," Pop said.

"Help! Put me down!" hollered Piers. "PUT ME DOWN!"

Chapter 7

"YOU KNOW how to play chess?" Garrett asked.

"Well now, it's been years," Pop replied. "But I still remember how the pieces move."

"Can you show me?"

"What is it that you want Pop to show you?" Gram cut in. She had returned with an ice pack. Garrett put the pawn back in the box, took the ice pack, and placed it on his head.

"Thanks, Gram," Garrett smiled. "I'd like Pop to show me how these pieces move."

"Can you believe it?" Pop asked incredulously. "Garrett found this set under my workbench."

Gram looked it over and wrinkled her nose. "Before you and Pop do anything, that box needs a good dusting. And we need to get you cleaned up. How's your head feeling?"

"The ice is helping," Garrett told her.

"Well, to be on the safe side, let's skip going out to eat. I'll make a nice pot of spaghetti and you can rest."

"And play chess with Pop?"

"Later. After dinner," Gram said.

Back in the box, Piers let out a sigh of relief. Then the pawn exploded.

"Um, excuse me, but DID ANY OF YOU SEE WHAT JUST HAPPENED? Did anyone notice that I was taken from our box and held in a TERRIFYING GRIP OF DEATH by that giant? Would someone PLEASE tell me what's going on?"

Bishop Preston was the first to speak.

"You weren't in any danger, Piers," he said.

"But...I...death...the Giant..." spluttered Piers.

"Piers, you are a chess piece," Bishop Preston reminded him.

"I know THAT," Piers retorted. "Just like all of you. But what does that have to do with anything?"

"Piers, do you know what it is that chess pieces do?" the bishop asked softly.

"Well, we live in the box together," replied Piers.

The other pieces began to chuckle, but Bishop Preston gave them a stern glance, and the laughter ceased immediately.

"Now listen. All of you know why Piers didn't give the right answer to my question," admonished the bishop. "You all know what happened. In the beginning. So many years ago."

"That's true," said Bishop Kirby. "And I think Piers needs to know now, too."

"What do I need to know?" asked Piers. "What is the mystery here?"

"I'll tell him," Parker offered. "I remember it like it was yesterday."

"Start with the farmer's workbench!" suggested Penelope.

"No. You need to go back farther," corrected Phoebe. "Start with the tree."

King George raised his hand for silence.

"We need to start at the beginning. Before the workbench. Before the tree. Piers, before all of those things, there was a wish...."

Chapter 8

AFTER a few hours had passed, Garrett felt much better. He didn't have a headache. The scratches on his arms were beginning to fade. And Gram's spaghetti had 'hit the spot.' (Pop always said that after one of Gram's meals.)

Garrett and Pop were just finishing bowls of chocolate ice cream when Gram set the wooden box on the table. It looked completely different now. She had dusted it, and the dark wood grain shone brilliantly.

"But not too late," she reminded Garrett. "Your parents are picking you up early tomorrow morning, so you need to get a good night's sleep."

King George cleared his throat and began the tale—

A very long time ago, a farmer lived here with his wife and their young son. One winter, there was a record-breaking streak of snowstorms. At first, the family enjoyed the snow very much. They built forts and had snowball fights. But after the fourth or fifth storm, the snow had gotten so deep that the family couldn't even open the front door. They were stuck inside the house for days on end. The family read books and had long conversations. They cleaned every room and cooked some delicious meals. But they soon grew weary of all that.

"I wish we had a game to play together," sighed the boy one evening after they had read their favorite book for the third time.

"Me too," agreed the farmer. "The next time we are in town, we will buy some board games at the store."

Two days later, the worst blizzard of all arrived. Not only was it impossible to open the door, the family couldn't even see out of the windows! Because they couldn't go outside, and because they had read every last book, there was nothing else to do but go to bed after dinner.

The storm raged on, and in the middle of the night the family heard a thunderous crack! Several days later, when some of the snow finally melted and they could see outside, they realized that a huge branch had snapped off the butternut tree in the front yard.

"Well, look at that, son!" exclaimed the farmer. He and his son gazed at the downed limb. "Your wish has come true!"

The farmer's son didn't know what his father was talking about. He had wished for a board game, not a fallen tree branch. But the farmer had an idea. He and his son shoveled a path to the branch, then trudged through the snow to the toolshed dragging the branch behind them. For the next few months, the farmer and the son whittled a set of wooden chess pieces from the branch. Two kings. Two queens. Four bishops. Four knights. Four rooks. Sixteen pawns. Once the whittling was completed, they painted half the pieces white and the other half black.

Finally the chess set was ready. It had taken six months to create.

In addition to the pieces, the farmer had also built a wooden box with metal hinges to store the pieces. The box itself was unusual—when it was opened, the farmer would spin it, and it became the chess board!

Summer had arrived by this time, and the farmer and his son planned to play their first game on the picnic table in the yard.

The son was more excited than he had ever been in his life. He was running from the toolshed to the picnic table, swinging the box in his hands, when, without warning, he tripped! As he fell to the ground, the box flew into the air. As the box hit the ground, the latch sprung open and the pieces flew in all directions!

Other than a skinned knee, the son was unhurt. He stood up, gathered the pieces, and placed them back in the box. However when he and the farmer set them up on the board later, they quickly realized that one was missing.

A white pawn.

The son was heartbroken. He and his father searched in the grass until dark, but there was no sign of it.

"How can we play?" the son cried. "The set is ruined!"

"We can still play," the farmer reassured him. He reached into his pocket and pulled out a coin. It was a shiny copper penny. "We will use this penny in place of the pawn until it turns up." Then they went into the house and played their first game.

For many years after, the farmer and his son used the penny in place of the pawn.

The farmer's son got very good at chess. So good that the farmer bought a fancier set for him when the boy left for college—a set with glass pieces. The son packed it up with his books.

The most remarkable thing happened a week after the son left for college. The farmer was building a shelf in the toolshed when he dropped a screw. It rolled under the workbench. When he reached down to grab it, he got the surprise of his life. The lost white pawn was lying there! It had never been in the box to begin with!

The farmer returned the pawn to the wooden box with the other pieces and stored it back beneath the workbench. He planned to surprise his son with the complete set when he came home.

But he never did. When the son returned, he took out the glass set and they played on that one. And for years and years, the whittled, wooden set remained unused under the workbench.

Until....

Chapter 9

"EVEN the box is beautiful," Pop murmured. "Carved by hand, I believe."

He sat staring at it.

The box was certainly unusual.

But Garrett wanted to learn about the pieces.

"Okay, let's see what I remember," Pop told him.

He released the latch.

"I remember now," whispered Piers. "I was that lost pawn. I slipped out of the farmer's hands as he was placing us into the box, and I rolled away underneath the workbench."

"I remember the day you were found!" recalled Portia. "What a surprise it was when our box's lid opened and you were dropped in!"

"We were finally a complete set again," nodded Pippa. She immediately felt badly for saying that. The penny was still in the box, and she hoped its feelings weren't hurt.

"And that's why you have never participated in a game," King George explained to Piers. "You see, we wait in the box until a human opens the lid. And then, when they do...."

"It's time for battle!" declared Sir Nicholas.

"Don't get ahead of yourself," Bishop Reginalt said. "First we assume our battle positions on the board."

"He means that the humans place us on our squares," added Kenfig Castle.

All of the pieces began chiming in.

"It's soooo exciting!"

"Thrilling!"

"A little nerve-wracking if you ask me!"

"But yes, the game begins as soon as we are all set up," King George went on. "A white piece is always moved first."

"Why?" asked Piers.

"It's the rule," replied Calvay Castle.

"Does it hurt?" inquired Piers.

"Does what hurt, dear?" asked Queen Nora.

"Being moved around the board. It sounds a little scary."

All of the pieces burst into laughter but were quickly silenced with a stern look from King George.

"Certainly not," he informed Piers. "It's all very orderly and actually quite fun. The humans pick us up. Then they place us down on a different square. It's as easy as—" Then the King was abruptly cut off by a blinding flash of light.

The humans had opened the box!

Chapter 10

POP ROTATED the wooden box, and all of the pieces rolled around.

"Well now, look at this!" he exclaimed. "A hand-painted board! And it's part of the box, too! Amazing!" He gazed at it for a long moment, admiring the craftsmanship. "Remember that the board should always be positioned like this," he instructed Garrett. "With the white square in the bottom right-hand corner."

Garrett nodded. "Okay."

Pop reached in and grabbed a tall black piece with a crown on top.

"This is a queen. The queen is the most powerful piece on the board," he said. "She always sits on her color, looking at the center two squares in the last row." He placed the queen on the black square on Garrett's side of the board. "Now see here. The queen can move all over the board, as many squares as she wants. Up, down, left, right.

She can even move diagonally." Pop demonstrated this, moving her around the board. Then he reached in and took out the other queen. "This is the white one. She also goes on her color, on the opposite side." Pop placed her on the appropriate white square. Now the two powerful pieces were facing each other from across the board.

"Is this the King?" Garrett asked. He had picked up a taller black piece. It had a crown with a cross on top that kind of looked like a plus sign.

"That's right," Pop replied. "Each king goes next to its queen." He pointed to the square on the board, and Garrett placed it there. Then he picked up the white king and placed it next to the white queen. "The king can only move one square at a time in any direction."

"Well, that's kind of boring," Garrett decided. "I mean, compared to the queen."

"I suppose so," Pop said. "It does take the king a long time to get anywhere."

"What are these pieces?" Garrett asked. "They look like castles."

"Those are the rooks. Each side has two, and they go here." Pop took the two black rooks and placed each one on the corner squares on Garrett's back row. Then he placed the two white rooks on his own corner squares. "Rooks are pretty powerful. They can move horizontally and vertically as far as they want."

Garrett reached into the box for two more pieces.

"Horses!" he exclaimed.

"Those are called knights," Pop corrected. "They sit next to each rook." He placed all of the knights on the board. "They are the only pieces that can jump over other pieces, and they move in an L pattern. One up and two over. Or two up and one over, which is pretty much the same thing. They move over a total of three squares each time." He demonstrated with a white knight.

"Cool!" smiled Garrett. He couldn't wait to use the knights.

There were only four tall pieces left. They all had pointy heads.

"These are bishops," Pop said. "Each bishop stands on the square next to a knight. They can move diagonally as far as they want, but they have to stay on the color that they started on." He demonstrated what diagonally meant as he moved one of the white bishops around the board.

Garrett noticed there were still plenty of pieces in the box. They were small and, other than half of them being black and the other half white, they all looked the same.

Pop picked up a random handful. "Last but not least, these are the pawns. There will be eight on your side and eight on mine. Each pawn stands in front of a piece. They can move two spaces forward on their first move, and one space at a time after that. But they can't capture pieces when they forward. They can only capture diagonally."

"Wow," sighed Garrett. "There sure is a lot to remember."

"That's true. It's impossible to learn everything all at once. Now the *best* thing about pawns is that—"

CRASH!

"What in the world was THAT?!" cried Pop.

King George was right—being picked up by a human was an odd sensation. But it didn't hurt at all.

Piers was now standing on a square in front of a knight. He couldn't help wondering what was going to happen next.

He was also wondering about what the human had been saying. What was the best thing about pawns?

He really wanted to know!

Chapter 11

"EVERYTHING'S OKAY!" called Gram. "I was just drying the spaghetti pot and it slipped out of my hands!"

Pop rose from his chair. "I'd better go give Gram a hand. And you'd best get some shut-eye."

He and Garrett scooped up the pieces and placed them back inside the wooden box.

"Thanks so much for teaching me about chess," Garrett said. "I can't wait to play!"

"Why don't you take the set home with you?" Pop suggested. "Maybe you can play a game with some of your friends."

A smile lit up Garrett's face. "I'd love to—if you're sure you really don't *want* the set, that is."

"Gram will be very happy if you take it home," Pop reassured him. "It will be one less thing to pack."

The pieces were back in the box now.

It was dark.

Again.

Piers was upset.

Just when he thought he would be in a game, the humans had called it off.

He was also puzzled.

"What did that human mean?" he called out.

"About getting some shut-eye?" asked Queen Beatrice. "That means that the humans are going to sleep."

"No," clarified Piers. "He was just about to say what the best thing was about pawns. What is the best thing about pawns?"

"Nothing!" snickered Sir John.

"How impolite!" gasped Queen Nora.

"But everyone knows that knights are the best!" proclaimed Sir John. "We are brave! We are daring! What other pieces can say that they are able to jump all over the board on magnificent steeds?"

"Jumping's not all that great," contradicted Stirling Castle.

"Rooks are clearly the best. We are solid! We are fortresses! What other pieces are able to say that they are architectural wonders?"

The other knights and rooks joined in the fray.

"Knights are the best!"

"No! Rooks!"

The four bishops tried to calm them down, but no one was listening.

The arguing grew louder and louder until King Edward called for silence.

"Cease this bickering at once!" he commanded. "I will not stand for it!"

"Nor will I," added King George. "These are peaceable kingdoms."

"If you had all been paying closer attention," Bishop Kirby began, "you would have heard that the human was not saying that a certain piece was the best. He was just about to say what the best thing about pawns was. He was simply extolling the virtues of the pawns."

"Each piece is necessary," added Queen Nora. "Every piece has an important job."

It grew very quiet in the box.

Sir John felt ashamed. Quite dishonorable. Quite un-knightly. He knew what he must do.

"I apologize to one and all," he stated. "But mostly to Piers.

There is something important and unique about each of us."

"That was most noble and humble, Sir John," King Edward told him.

"Yes, thank you, Sir John," Piers added.

"Now, I suggest that we all get some shut-eye," said Queen Beatrice. "I have a feeling that things are about to get quite exciting for all of us in the days ahead."

The pieces slowly drifted off to sleep.

All except Piers.

He thought about what Sir John had said. Each piece was important and unique. That was true.

But he also couldn't help thinking about what the human had said.

'Now the best thing about pawns is—'

He was puzzled.

What was the best thing?

What was it?

He had to find out. He just had to.

Chapter 12

"SO, DID YOU have fun with Gram and Pop?" Mom asked Garrett as he sat in the back of the car, playing a game on his phone.

Garrett looked up.

"It was great but—"

"But what?"

"It's just that...well...I'm really sad that it was my last visit to the farm," he replied. "I'll never see Josh or Max again." A lump formed in his throat, and he felt like he was going to cry.

Garrett's dad, who was driving, took his eyes off the road just long enough to look at him in the rearview mirror.

"We're all going to miss that place," he agreed, nodding. "I grew up there, and that place holds a lot of good memories."

"You didn't own a chess set when you lived there, did you, dad?"

His dad brought the car to a stop at a red light.

"A chess set? No, why?"

"Because I found one underneath Pop's workbench. It's in here." He held up the wooden box so his parents could see it.

"Well, it's not mine," his dad said. "I had checkers and Scrabble, but not chess."

"A chess set?" asked Mom. "I was wondering what Gram and Pop had sent you home with."

"Pop showed me how the pieces move," he told them. "I'm going to take the set to school tomorrow and see if anyone wants to play."

The light turned green, and his dad grinned at his mom as he stepped on the gas.

"You never know," he said. "The next grandmaster just might be in the backseat!"

"We're going to school!" reported Peri. She had been listening through a crack near the box's hinge.

All of the pieces began talking at once.

It was very exciting indeed.

Chapter 13

GARRETT'S BACKPACK was heavier and lumpier than usual with the chess set inside it. Myles, his best friend, noticed this right away.

"Whatcha got in there?" he asked as they were getting on the bus. "Smokey?"

Myles laughed. They were always talking about how much fun it would be to sneak Garrett's dog, Smokey, into school for a day.

"Wait until I show you. I found a really old chess set underneath my Pop's workbench this weekend," Garrett said. He unzipped his backpack so that Myles could see the wooden box.

"Whoa, that's cool," Myles replied. "How old do you think it is? How much do you think it's worth?"

Garrett could see where the conversation was going. Myles's mom was a 'flipper.' She was always picking up furniture that people were throwing away. Many times she would be driving Garrett and Myles to soccer practice and they'd find themselves squished next to some old table or cabinet. She would paint what she called her "treasures" and sell them at flea markets. Myles said she made quite a lot of money flipping furniture.

"I'm not selling this set. I'm keeping it," Garrett told him. "But I need to find someone to teach me how to play."

Skylah, who was in the seat in front of them, turned around.

"Not that I'm eavesdropping or anything," she said. "But I can help you with that."

"Do you know how to play chess?" asked Garrett.

"No," she replied. "But I know someone who does. Meet me in the library during recess."

The pieces heard all sorts of sounds in school—

"Who can find the perimeter of this shape?"

"Today we are going to read Chapter Three."

"Mrs. Thompson, can I go to the bathroom?"

And then, all of a sudden, it grew very quiet....

Chapter 14

THE LIBRARY was always open during recess. A handful of students were relaxing on beanbag chairs with their noses buried in books. Almost all the computer stations were occupied. Two of the students were working on a puzzle. Another, wearing a badge that said LIBRARY HELPER, was feeding the fish in a large tank.

Garrett looked all around but did not see Myles or Skylah.

"Can I help you?"

It was Ms. Kimberly, the librarian. She spoke in a hushed voice.   .

"I'm looking for Skylah," Garrett whispered back. "She said to meet her here because she knows someone who plays chess."

"Ah, chess," smiled Ms. Kimberly. "The Game of Kings. 794."

"794?" asked Garrett.

A dreamy look came over the librarian's face.

"Section 794. Indoor games of skill," she murmured.

Garrett knew what was coming next; the same thing that always happened when Ms. Kimberly started thinking about the Dewey Decimal system. She *loved* the way books were organized.

Ms. Kimberly looked Garrett squarely in the eye.

"I will lead you to the chess books."

The next thing Garrett knew he was following Ms. Kimberly as she wound her way through the stacks of books. He almost ran into her when she halted abruptly at the 700s. Then she pointed to a spot on the shelf.

"794.2. Checkers. 794.6. Indoor bowling. And here we are…794.1. Chess!"

She smiled broadly as she began pulling books from the shelves and holding them out to him.

"Now let's see what we have here…*How to Play Chess, Chess Openings for Kids, Play Better Chess Today*…."

Skylah and Myles had entered the library and were waving to Garrett from across the room.

"Um, excuse me, Ms. Kimberly," he said, feeling terrible for interrupting her. She was holding up *Chess Puzzles for Kids*. "I have to go. My friends are here. You see,

I'm not really looking for a book about chess. I'm looking for a person to play chess *with*."

Ms. Kimberly smiled.

"Well, all of the grandmasters read books about chess. You know, to learn about the moves and tactics. So if you change your mind, you know where they are—here at 794.1."

"Thanks, Ms. Kimberly," Garrett said. Then he walked over and joined Skylah and Myles.

"Sorry we're late," Myles told him.

"It was Mr. S," Skylah explained. "He was going on and on about Mesopotamia."

"The bell rang and it was like he didn't even notice," Myles added. "None of us were allowed to leave until we guessed the Sumerians' most important invention. It took like *fifty* guesses before Brandon yelled out '*THE WHEEL!*'"

"I didn't think we'd ever escape!" Skylah said.

She and Myles started cracking up. Ms. Kimberly shushed them, and Skylah mouthed a silent *Sorry*.

Garrett held up the wooden box to remind them why they were here.

"Oh yeah, the chess set!" Skylah whispered. She

looked around the library. "I know he's in here. We just have to find him."

"Who?" Garrett asked. "Who is it we're looking for?"

"Beamer," she replied.

The pieces all agreed that it would have been great to actually see Ms. Kimberly. They had learned so much just by listening to her. But they had many more questions, too.

They all began whispering in the dark—

"What is checkers?"

"What is bowling?"

"What are tactics?"

No one knew.

"There's one thing I do know, however," announced King Edward. "A game is in our future!"

They had waited so long. It had seemed like it would never happen. It was a dream come true.

"Huzzah!" cried the pieces.

Chapter 15

BEAMER, thought Garrett. *Great....*

Beamer was a legend in their school.

In first grade, he won the spelling bee.

In second grade, during the annual talent show, he recited the names of all the presidents in under two minutes.

In third grade, he hit a grand slam to win the game that sent his team to the Little League World Series.

In fourth grade, he earned his blackbelt in karate.

And now, in fifth grade, he had set a goal for himself—he was going to audition for the TV show *How Smart Are You? Kids Version.* That was why when Garrett, Skylah, and Myles found him, he was sitting at the back of the library reading a book about Australia. He was trying to memorize its states and territories.

"Hey Beamer," Skylah said. She pulled out a chair and sat down next to him.

Beamer lifted his eyes from the Australia book.

"G'day mates," he replied. "That's how they say hello in Australia." Then he saw the wooden box. "What's that?"

"It's a chess set," Garrett said. "Skylah says you know how to play."

"Yes, I've been playing since I was five," Beamer replied. "Sometimes my mom takes me into the city on the weekends to play at Chess Corner."

"With other kids?" Myles asked.

"With anyone who knows how to play. It doesn't matter how old you are. Can I see the set?"

Garrett held the box out to him.

"Sweet," whistled Beamer. He opened it and dumped the pieces onto the table. They rolled around noisily. Then he spun the box so the board opened. "These pieces are nice. They look handmade."

"I know how to set up the board, and I've got a basic idea of how the pieces move," Garrett told him.

"Then let's play. Black or white?"

Garrett remembered what Pop had said. White always went first. Maybe he should let Beamer be white, he thought. After all, he *was* showing him how to play.

"You can be white," Garrett said.

Everyone became quite dizzy after they crashed onto the table and rolled around, so it felt good settling onto their squares.

Piers was confused though. He was on the square in front of Queen Nora.

"Um, I think I'm in the wrong spot!" he called out. "No offense Your Majesty, but last time I stood in front of a knight."

Sir John let out a chuckle.

"Pawns don't have designated spots," he informed Piers.

Phinian, who was next to Piers in front of King Edward, stood up straighter.

"Neither do you, Sir John," Phinian pointed out. "You can be queenside or kingside." He turned to Piers. "You aren't necessarily placed on the same square at the start of every game. There are eight different starting positions. It's actually quite exciting for us pawns!"

Piers was puzzled. Was that the best thing about pawns? he wondered. Starting in a new square each game?

He didn't have time to think about it now, though—Phinian had just been moved!

Chapter 16

BEAMER BEGAN the game by moving his king's pawn ahead two spaces.

"Pawn to e4," said Beamer.

"Wait, what's e4?" asked Garrett. "What does that mean?"

"The chess board is a grid," Beamer replied. He went on to explain the system of letters and numbers that defined each square.

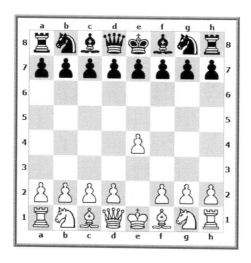

"It reminds me of the game, Battleship," Skylah said.

"They're definitely similar in that way," Beamer told her, nodding.

Garrett remembered what Pop had said about pawns and how they could move up two spaces on the first move. So he copied Beamer by moving his king's pawn to e5. Now the two pawns faced each other in the center of the board.

Beamer slid his queen diagonally all the way to the h5 square.

Garrett hadn't expected such a bold move. He knew the queen was a powerful piece and sensed he was in trouble. He looked to Skylah and Myles for help, but they only shrugged their shoulders.

"We're learning just like you," Myles said.

Garrett remembered that the king could only move up one space, so he moved his king to e7.

This turned out to be a grave mistake.

Beamer moved his queen quickly and took Garrett's pawn on e5.

"That's checkmate, mates," he said.

"What does that mean?" asked Garrett.

"It means the game's over," Beamer replied. "Now we

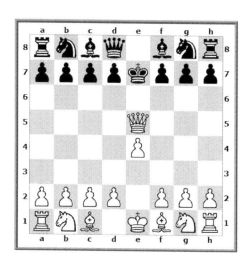

shake hands."

"Already?" cried Garrett.

"Well, your king can't move two squares to capture my queen. None of your pieces can block the queen. And no matter where you try to move your king, he will still be in check," he explained. "So like I said, that's checkmate."

Garrett reached across and shook Beamer's hand.

"It just went so quickly," Garrett sighed.

"Don't feel bad," Beamer consoled him. "I lost a lot of games when I first started playing. That's normal."

The bell rang to signal that recess was over. Garrett and Beamer placed the pieces back inside the box.

"Thanks, Beamer," Garrett said.

Beamer smiled. "Bring your set in again sometime." He, Skylah, and Myles began moving toward the library door, but Garrett hung back.

"Aren't you coming?" asked Skylah. They all had math together next period.

"I'll be there in a minute," Garrett told her.

He walked over to the circulation desk, where Ms. Kimberly was putting labels onto the spines of books.

"Ms. Kimberly… um…about those chess books."

Ms. Kimberly reached under the desk and brought out the same books she'd been showing him earlier. She handed them over with a grin.

"I knew you'd be back for them."

Piers couldn't believe how quickly it had all happened.

In the box.

Out of the box.

And now back in the box.

"I've always hoped to be moved first, and today it finally happened!" exclaimed Phinian.

"And not just one space, but two!" added Philip. "It was certainly your lucky day!"

"How thrilling it was to glide across the board again," sighed Queen Nora. "I find moving diagonally so elegant."

"I knew I shouldn't have moved forward," remarked King George. "Garrett has a lot to learn."

"Well, you can't possibly compare him to Beamer. That young man is brilliant," said King Edward.

"Everyone was once a beginner," Bishop Preston reminded everyone. "I have a feeling Garrett will develop into a fine player. He's very curious about the game."

Piers was very quiet. He was somewhat disappointed. He hadn't been moved at all. But to be fair, most of the other pieces—including the rooks, bishops and knights—hadn't moved, either.

"Are all games like this one?" Piers asked.

"No, each game is different," replied Bishop Channing. "That's the beauty of chess. There are so many possibilities. In one game you might stand in your starting position waiting for hours to be moved, and in the next game you could be all over the board. No two games are ever the same."

Piers felt reassured hearing that.

Hopefully he'd see more action next time!

Chapter 17

"YOUR BACKPACK is even larger than it was this morning," Myles remarked. He'd almost been whacked in the head by it as he and Garrett got onto the bus after school.

"Yeah, I checked out a bunch of books about chess from the library."

"Extra reading? You're crazy!"

"I just want to learn the game," Garrett replied. He plopped down onto the seat with the overstuffed backpack on his lap. "And...maybe not right away...but maybe someday I'll...." he trailed off.

"Someday you'll what?" asked Myles.

Garrett lowered his voice to a whisper. "Maybe I'll beat Beamer someday."

Skylah's head popped up from the seat in front of them and turned around.

"Not that I'm eavesdropping or anything, but you

want to beat Beamer at chess? Are you serious?"

"Good grief! Are you *always* listening to us?" Myles asked.

"Yes," replied Skylah. "I find your conversations extremely fascinating."

Myles rolled his eyes.

"I know beating Beamer is a long shot," Garrett said. "Maybe I just want to get good enough to put his king in check. The thing is, this set was hidden under my Pop's workbench for a really long time. I think I was meant to rescue it or something. And I know this is going to sound weird but…I feel like I owe it to the pieces to become a good player."

Myles and Skylah stared at him.

"You did hear Beamer say that he's been playing since he was five, right?" Skylah asked.

"Yeah, but there are lots of people who start out later in life and do great things," Garrett pointed out. "We just learned about that painter, Grandma Moses, in Art class the other day. She didn't start painting until she was 78!"

"True," Myles agreed. He was in the same art class.

"*And*, you know that guy who played Han Solo in *Star Wars*?" Garrett went on.

"Harrison Ford?"

"Yeah. He was in his thirties when he got the part. And I'm only eleven. My whole life is ahead of me."

Skylah shook her head. "It's going to be a lot of work."

"I know. And that's why I need help."

He stared at Myles.

"Me?" Myles asked, clearly surprised. "How can *I* help?"

"You can be my coach."

"But I know less about chess than *you* do!"

"Well then, maybe not my coach, but you can pump me up with positivity," smiled Garrett. "You can be my moral support."

"And I'll be your manager," Skylah stated.

"Um, what would that require, exactly?" Garrett asked.

"I'll line up people for you to practice with. And I'll be in charge of your schedule."

Garrett thought it over, then smiled. "Sounds like a good deal. You'll do it for free, right?"

"My services are free of charge. And another thing—if the three of us are going to be working together, we need a name."

"A name?" asked Myles. "What kind of a name? The

Beat Beamer Club?"

"No. I've been thinking of it ever since recess. Beamer said, 'That's checkmate, mates.' We should call ourselves 'Checkmates'."

"Checkmates," nodded Garrett. "I like it."

The sound of clanking and clanging woke Piers up.

"What's going on?" he cried.

"It's the knights," Porter explained. "They're cleaning their weapons and armor."

"I don't recall them doing that before," Piers said. "I mean, they never did it when our box was under the workbench."

"Those were years without battles. But times are changing."

"We must always be ready to defend our kings!" shouted Dame Mary.

"We must stay physically strong!" added Sir Nicholas. "Therefore I propose a few rounds of push-ups and sit-ups when we've finished sharpening our swords!"

"And after that, I propose horse vaulting!" announced Sir John. "And somersaults!"

"And let us finish up with punching practice!" called out Sir Charles.

"Huzzah!" cried the knights.

"Punching practice?" inquired Piers. "What does that mean?"

He thought it sounded a little worrisome and possibly dangerous.

"The knights punch the ground or the walls to toughen their hands," Porter told him.

"Will there be another battle soon?" asked Piers.

"It appears so," replied Porter. "It really does appear so."

Chapter 18

THREE DAYS later, Skylah asked for permission to sit in Calliope's seat on the bus.

"I know *for a fact* that Calliope is going to be gone for two weeks," she informed Frank, the bus driver. "Her family is on vacation. They are going spelunking. Spelunking is—"

"I'm sure spelunking is very interesting," Frank cut in. "But we've got to get a move on or you're all going to be late to school. I heard there's traffic downtown."

"Sooooo…does that mean I can sit in Calliope's seat?"

Frank nodded. "Fine, fine," he said, waving her away. "But don't make a big deal and go announcing it. I don't want every kid on this bus playing musical seats."

"You're the best, Frank!" Skylah smiled, and she almost skipped down the aisle to her new seat. (Secretly she was hoping that Calliope would agree to switch seats permanently when she got back.)

The reason Skylah wanted Calliope's seat was because it was directly across from Garrett and Myles. Her neck had been growing sore from twisting around to talk with them in her old seat. And today she really needed to talk.

"Hi Checkmates!" she exclaimed when she sat down. "I need to speak with you."

"What's up with the get-up?" laughed Myles. "You look like...I don't know...maybe like a reporter, or a teacher, or something."

Skylah was holding a spiral notebook and a pen. Fashion glasses were perched on the end of her nose. She frowned over the rims of the glasses at Myles.

"I'm calling this meeting to order," she announced, tapping the notebook with her pen. "I have two weeks' worth of practice games lined up for you," she said directly to Garrett. "The first one is after school today."

"Let me see that," Garrett said, pointing. Skylah handed him the notebook. Then, "You scheduled me for all of these games?" he asked incredulously. "How did you find all of these people? How do you even know that they *play* chess?"

Skylah pointed proudly to the button on her shirt that said *Play Chess???*

"Your first game is at four o'clock today with my Aunt Lu," Skylah said. "She has to work at the Mainstreet Market, but I convinced her to play during her dinner break. So don't take the bus home. We're walking there after school."

"I'm going to have to let my mom know where I'll be," Garrett pointed out.

"Me too," added Myles.

"Already taken care of," Skylah told them. "My mom is going to pick us up after the game at five and drive you home. She emailed your moms last night, and they said it was fine."

"I can't believe you set all this up," Garrett said, shaking his head. "It's pretty amazing."

"I *am* your manager," Skylah shrugged. "See you after school!"

"If only we had some stones to throw," Sir John lamented. "It would help build our upper body strength."

"Well, maybe there's something else we could throw," Sir Nicholas suggested.

"Maybe we could throw the pawns," said Sir Charles. "We can see how far we can throw them."

"Or how many we can throw at a time," added Dame Mary.

"Throwing the bishops would be better," Sir John went on. "They are slightly taller."

"Certainly not!" Queen Nora scolded.

"Throwing any piece is strictly forbidden," Queen Beatrice agreed.

"It's the most ridiculous thing I've ever heard of," Queen Nora snorted.

"But we must continue preparing for battle," Sir Nicholas argued. "What do you think we should do?"

"Might I suggest a jog around the box?" Queen Beatrice asked.

"A brilliant idea, Your Majesty!" said Sir John with a bow.

Then he and the knights took off running, their armor clanging with each step.

Chapter 19

"NOW, I only have an hour," said Aunt Lu as she led the Checkmates to the breakroom at the back of the Mainstreet Market. She hung her apron on a hook, walked over to a white refrigerator, and removed a red canvas lunch sack.

"I'm going to heat up some leftovers, but you kids are welcome to have some snacks," she told them.

She pulled a container out of her sack, popped it into the microwave, and set the timer for two minutes. Soon the room began to smell quite garlicky.

"Go on, help yourselves," she prodded.

A large, plastic basket on the table was filled to the brim with packaged snacks. Garrett and Myles opened bags of potato chips, and Skylah ripped open a package of chocolate chip cookies. While they were munching, Garrett set the wooden box on the table and began setting up the chess pieces.

Moments later, Aunt Lu sat down across from him. She opened her food container and steam wafted out. She stuck her fork in and began eating garlic chicken.

"I can't say I've ever seen a set like this one," she remarked.

"I think it's pretty old and the pieces are probably hand carved," Garrett said. "It was hidden under my Pop's workbench for a long time."

"Well, the main thing is that you learn what to *do* with these pieces," Aunt Lu said. "You've got them all in the right spots. That's a good thing. Now, Skylah, hide a black and white pawn behind your back. Then Garrett can choose a hand. That's how we'll decide who is black and white."

Skylah followed Aunt Lu's instructions and held out her fists.

Garrett pointed to the right one.

Skylah opened her hand—there was a white pawn in her palm.

"Okay, here we go!" smiled Aunt Lu.

Garrett picked up the pawn in front of his queen and was about to move it.

"Wait!" cried Skylah.

"What's wrong?" asked Myles.

"You!" Skylah said to him. "You are Garrett's moral support. You need to pump him up!"

Myles patted Garrett on the shoulder and smiled.

"Good luck, man. You got this."

"Next time you need to make a banner or a sign or something," Skylah added.

"Enough fooling around," said Aunt Lu. "Now I have less than an hour."

Garrett moved his queen's pawn ahead two spaces.

Aunt Lu moved her king's knight to f6.

Garrett moved his king's pawn ahead two spaces.

Aunt Lu frowned. She took that pawn with her knight.

"Let's stop for a minute," she said. "You do realize

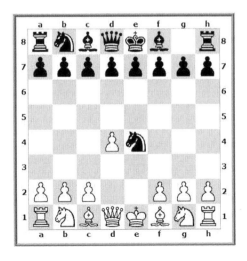

you left that pawn unprotected, right?"

"What do you mean?" Garrett asked.

"Garrett, defense is really important when you are playing chess. When you move a piece, you need to think about what my next move might be," she explained. "And if you think that I might take your piece, that piece has to be protected."

"Ohhh," murmured Garrett. "I hadn't really thought about that."

"I can see we have some work before we go any further," smiled Aunt Lu.

"I don't think this game is going to continue," Portia said.

"All that training for nothing," lamented Sir Nicholas.

"I think it's just going to be a long conversation about defending pieces, but it is necessary," Bishop Reginalt explained.

Bishop Channing nodded in agreement.

"If Garrett doesn't learn how to protect his pieces, he will never beat Beamer," she stated.

Chapter 20

IT WAS TRUE.

Aunt Lu had ended the game after only four moves.

"It's more important for you to learn about defense," she said.

She moved some pawns into a diagonal line.

"A good example of defense is a pawn chain," she explained. "See? Each pawn protects the other. If a piece takes a pawn, the next pawn can take that piece, and so on."

Garrett nodded. It reminded him of his soccer team and how the fullbacks protected the goalie.

Piers had been in the pawn chain with Phoebe and Phinian.

Phoebe had been protecting Phinian, and he had been protecting Phoebe.

But who is protecting me? he wondered.

Castle Warwick stood firmly on the square behind him.

"Don't worry, I am defending you," stated the rook.

It all seemed very important, and Piers wondered if being in a pawn chain was the best thing about pawns....

Chapter 21

"SORRY TO bother you on your break, but I need your help, Lu."

Mike, the manager of the Mainstreet Market stood in the doorway of the breakroom. He had a troubled look on his face.

"Hey kids," he said. "We're in a bit of a pickle. Jane just got a call from her son. Seems he ran out of gas out on the highway, and she has to run out and pick him up. So Lu, can you take her place on the register until she gets back?"

"No problem, Mike." Aunt Lu stood up from the table. "Sorry kids, but we'll have to continue another time."

"I really appreciate you teaching me about defense," Garrett said. "And pawn chains."

Aunt Lu put her apron back on.

"Rome wasn't built in a day," she said, "and neither are great chess players. You'll get the hang of it."

"My mom won't be here till five o'clock," Skylah said. "You know, to pick us up."

"No worries," Aunt Lu replied. "You're welcome to hang out in here and enjoy the snacks."

Skylah smiled. "You're the best, Aunt Lu."

Life had certainly gotten busier than ever for the pieces.

It had been dark and still for years on end when the box was underneath the workbench. But now there seemed to be something going on almost every day. Often they would have just settled down to sleep when the box would suddenly lurch and they'd all tumble on top of each other.

"Why must Garrett be such an early riser?" asked Warwick Castle. "I require a good deal of rest, you know. With all I must do to secure the fortress each night—raising the drawbridge, closing the windows, and locking the doors—it is quite tiring. I fear we are only getting eight hours of sleep at most."

"It's because of school," Queen Nora replied. "School begins promptly in the morning. And Garrett brings us to school with him every day."

"I wonder where we're off to today?" Kenfig Castle mumbled. He was smushed underneath a pile of pawns.

"We shall see," replied King George. "We shall see."

Chapter 22

TWO DAYS LATER, Skylah slid into the seat across from the Garrett and Myles, who were engaged in a thumb-wrestling match.

"Hiya Checkmates! Are you ready for today?" She opened her notebook and tapped the point of the pen on the page.

Garrett looked over at the schedule. His momentary lapse in concentration gave Myles the advantage he needed. He quickly pinned Garret's thumb down with his own.

"Booyah!" Myles whooped.

Garrett pulled his hand away and wiggled his fingers. "Did I understand this correctly?" he asked Skylah. "The next game is at... *the animal shelter?*"

"Yup!" Skylah grinned broadly. "I had to make a deal with my neighbor, Mr. Jay, who works there."

"What kind of deal?"

"A barter. Cats for chess."

"Cats for chess?" Garrett echoed.

"While you are playing chess, Myles and I will be playing with the cats and filling their food and water dishes," she explained.

A huge smile broke out across Myles' face. He loved animals.

"Sweet," he said.

"What's that sound?" Piers asked.

"I can't be certain, but I think it's meowing," Bishop Channing replied. "I remember it from the toolshed."

"Remember how that cat used to claw at our box?" Queen Nora remembered. "It was a positively terrifying sound! I always worried that he'd get our box open and scratch us or pick one of us up in his mouth."

"Do not worry, Your Majesty!" declared Sir Nicholas. "We will protect you from any furry foes!"

"Huzzah!" cried the other knights.

A duel with a cat might be just as exciting as a battle on the chessboard!

Chapter 23

MR. JAY had just finished cleaning the last of seven litter boxes when the Checkmates walked through the front door of the animal shelter.

"Oh, you're here!" he smiled. "Excellent!"

The Checkmates gazed around the large room. Cats of all shapes, sizes, and colors were meandering about. Several kittens stared down at them from where they sat perched on cat-trees.

"I was just telling Myles and Garrett about our barter," Skylah said. "Cats for chess."

"I hope you don't mind, but it's going to have to be cats *and dogs* for chess," chuckled Mr. Jay. He pointed to a crate where two puppies with brown fur were curled up together. "Meet Mo and Molly. Brother and sister. The lady who is adopting them was supposed to pick them up this morning. But she called and said she couldn't come until later this evening. Can you two walk them around outside while we play? They could use some fresh air and a stretch."

"Oh yeah!" exclaimed Myles.

"Well then, I'll just put their leashes on...."

Mr. Jay bent down, unlatched the lock, and opened the door of the silver crate. The puppies bounded out and immediately began barking and jumping on him, their tails wagging furiously back and forth. Mr. Jay fastened the leashes onto their collars and handed one to Myles and the other to Skylah.

"You can walk them all around on the grass in the front," he instructed.

An orange-and-white-striped cat sauntered up to Garrett and began sniffing at the wooden box.

"Ah, now there's the set Skylah was telling me about," noted Mr. Jay. "Why don't you get us set up? We'll play right here." He motioned to a small card table with two folding chairs.

"Wait! I almost forgot!" exclaimed Myles. "One thing before we take the puppies out." He dug in his pocket and pulled out a folded piece of notebook paper, which he then handed it to Garrett.

"It's a motivational message," Myles grinned.

Garrett unfolded it and read the words Myles had hastily scrawled during his last class that day—

Good luck, Garrett! Don't lose.

"Thanks," said Garrett, placing the note on the table while Skylah and Myles headed out the door with the puppies.

As he began setting up the pieces, Garrett got the feeling that he was being watched. He looked up and saw a gray-and-black-striped kitten staring down at him from a cat-tree. Its tail twitched from left to right, and its yellow eyes followed every piece that Garrett put onto the board. Just as he was setting the final black pawn in place, the kitten leaped without warning from its resting place and landed—*thump!*—smack in the middle of the chess board!

The pieces bounced and rolled in all directions.

"It's a feline invasion!" cried Sir Nicholas.

"God save the Kings!" shouted Sir Charles. He drew his sword, flashing it in front of the kitten's nose. "Be off with you, thy monstrous beast!"

The kitten's eyes grew as round as saucers.

"Eioww!"

The creature pushed off the board with its hind legs, spun frantically in the air, and landed on the floor. Then it shot across the room and hid under a desk.

The pieces lay scattered and stunned.

"Is…the creature…gone?" whispered Queen Nora.

Sir Charles placed his sword back into its scabbard.

"You are safe, Your Majesty," he stated solemnly. "We all are."

Chapter 24

MR. JAY scooped up the pieces and began returning them to their places on the board.

"I am so sorry," he apologized. "That kitten is a maniac. I keep hoping someone will adopt him."

Then he looked at the board curiously.

"Oh dear, are we missing a pawn?"

The cat's tail had knocked Piers into the air, after which he bounced on the floor and rolled over and over until he came to a stop.

Now he lay under the table. It felt like he was stuck.

He couldn't believe his terrible luck.

He was separated from the other pieces.

Again.

Chapter 25

"IT'S GOT to be here," grunted Mr. Jay.

He and Garrett were on their hands and knees, searching for the lost pawn. An older calico cat wound its way around their arms and legs, purring loudly.

"It couldn't have gone far," Garrett said. He spied something white near one of the water dishes.

"There it—no, wait that's not it."

It was just a small ball. Garrett picked it up, and the bell inside it jingled. Then he tossed it to the calico cat.

"Got it!" shouted Mr. Jay. He scooted out from underneath the table with the pawn in his fist. "It was half-hidden under the radiator!"

Now Mr. Jay's pants were covered in cat hair, but he didn't seem to mind. He placed the pawn on the board in front of the white queen.

Garrett was relieved that Mr. Jay had found the pawn. He would've felt awful if he'd lost any of the pieces. His family had once put a five-hundred-piece jigsaw puzzle together, and when they'd finished it, they discovered that one piece was missing. It was really disappointing.

They sat down at the table.

"Black or white?" asked Mr. Jay.

"Black," replied Garrett.

"Where **were** you?" whispered Percipia. She was next to him, on the square in front of King Edward. "We were all getting really concerned."

"I rolled off the table after that...that...crazy cat attack," he whispered back. "And then I was stuck under a radiator. I didn't think anyone would find me."

"Well, thank goodness you're okay," Percipia smiled.

"Yes, glad you made it back," Peter added.

"It wouldn't be the same without you," Philbert called from across the board.

"I told you he'd be here before the game started," Prudence said. "You're all a bunch of worrywarts."

"Well, given Piers's history, I think we were right to be afraid," Pippa pointed out.

"And it's just not the same if one of us is missing," said Prentice.

Maybe that was the best thing about being a pawn, Piers thought—the fact that they worried about each other. And cared *about each other. And were glad that you were found after being lost.*

As much as Piers wanted to mull that thought over, he realized that it would have to wait until later. Mr. Jay had moved Percipia two spaces ahead to e4!

Chapter 26

"Hmm," murmured Garrett. He decided to open by moving his queenside knight to a6.

Mr. Jay pushed the king's pawn to e5.

Garrett then moved his queen's pawn ahead two spaces, to d5. The black and white pawns now stood next to each other.

Now Mr. Jay moved his king's pawn to d6 and took the pawn on d5.

"Wait a minute!" Garrett cried. "You can't do that!"

The door swung open, and Myles and Skylah came in with the two puppies. The puppies tugged on their leashes and headed in the direction of their food bowls.

"I think they're hungry," Skylah said. Then she looked from Mr. Jay to Garrett. Garrett was visibly upset.

"What's wrong?" she asked.

Garrett pointed across the board.

"He's cheating!" he shouted.

"What's going on?" Piers asked.

"It looks like Garrett is about to learn something new," Portia replied.

All of the pawns except Piers nodded and spoke in unison.

"En passant."

Chapter 27

"GARRETT!" Skylah exclaimed. "You need to calm down!"

"But...but he just—" Garrett sputtered, pointing at the board.

"Dude. I'm sure Mr. Jay wouldn't cheat," Myles said.

"Of course not," Mr. Jay said with a smile. "Why don't we all take a deep breath? Garrett, it looks like you're not aware of this very special chess move."

"What do you mean?" Garrett asked.

"Let's go back in time," said Mr. Jay. "You know that the game of chess has been around for centuries, right?"

"Like how many?" Myles asked.

"Well, people in India started playing in the *sixth* century," Garrett replied. "So that's about fifteen *hundred* years ago."

Myles and Skylah raised their eyebrows. "Whoa," Skylah said.

Garrett shrugged. "Yeah, I read it in one of the books that I checked out of the library."

"The sixth century is correct," nodded Mr. Jay. "But some of the rules in chess changed through the years. For example, the queen has become the most powerful piece on the board. And now players can castle to keep their king safe from—"

"Wait," interrupted Garrett. "Castle? What's that?"

"Castling is—well, I think it might be easier to show you, than tell you," Mr. Jay replied.

He removed the bishop and knight from in between his rook and king. Then he moved the king over two spots, and the rook 'jumped' the king so it was now on the other side of him. "Wow, that's cool!" Garrett smiled.

"You can castle on the king's side or queen's side, but you can only do it once in the game," Mr. Jay went on. "The king and rook must not have moved before, and you can only castle if the bishop and knight are out of the way. Also the king cannot pass through check during a castle. But overall, it's a great defensive move and helps keep the king protected."

"And what about that thing you did with the pawn before?" asked Garrett.

"Remember how I said that the game changed through the years?"

"Yeah."

"Well, around the time when the queen became the most powerful piece and castling began, some big changes began happening for the pawns, too. That's when they could move two spaces on their first move. Before that, they could only move ahead one square on the first move."

"This is really interesting," Skylah said.

"It really is. And that 'thing' I just did," Mr. Jay continued, "where I took your pawn is called *en passant.*"

"Sounds French," Myles decided.

"That's correct. It is a French expression that means 'in passing'. Now, just like castling, you can only make this move at certain times. It lets a pawn capture a pawn after it moves two spaces on its first move."

Mr. Jay demonstrated by setting two pawns—one of each color—on the board side by side.

"In this case," Mr. Jay said, "the pawn does not take the square of the one it captures. It *passes* the pawn as it captures it and lands on the space that was *behind* it. Each pawn only has one chance to make the en passant move—when it is already on the fifth line of squares, and one of the opponent's pawns moves two squares forward and comes alongside it. En passant isn't a very common move, but you should certainly know about it."

Garrett's brow furrowed. "It sounds pretty complicated. How did *you* learn all of this?"

"I read books, just like you, and got some of it from my father. Now, there's *one other special move for pawns....*" continued Mr. Jay.

Just as Garrett was leaning forward to hear about it, the door opened and a tall lady in high heels stepped inside.

"I'm here to pick up my little dah-lings!" she announced.

Mr. Jay stood up.

"I'm so sorry, but we'll have to cut this short," Mr. Jay said. "I've got some paperwork that must be filled out before Molly and Mo go home. So stop by another day and we can have a real game."

Garrett began placing the pieces back into the wooden box.

"This was really interesting and I learned a lot. Thanks so much."

"Can we stay and play with the cats for a little while?" Myles asked.

Mr. Jay handed each of them poles with feathers on the ends.

"Of course, he smiled. "Stay as long as you'd like."

Piers couldn't believe what he'd just heard.

The *information about how the rules had changed for pawns.*

Being able to move two spaces instead of just one.

And the en passant!

Wowee!

How fancy that sounded!

French!

And Mr. Jay had said that there was one more special move just for pawns.

If only that woman hadn't shown up, he would know what it was.

Whatever it was, it had to be the best thing about pawns.

He just knew it.

Chapter 28

SKYLAH LINED UP several other games for Garrett—

He played against the plumber who'd been fixing Skylah's mom's kitchen faucet.

He played against Skylah's cousin, Joey, who was in the second grade.

He played against Skylah's flute teacher after her flute lesson ended.

He played against Skylah's softball coach when her game was over. In that instance, they set the chessboard on the bench in the dugout and played until someone turned the lights out and the field became too dark.

He played against Greg, Skylah's drama teacher, after play practice. They sat on the floor of the stage while Skylah and Myles watched from the audience. They applauded each time Garrett called out "Check!" The game ended in a stalemate, which meant neither player won—it was a 'draw.' Garrett would have preferred to win, of course, but it was still better than losing!

"Not too shabby," Greg said, shaking Garrett's hand.

"I agree," Skylah added. "And speaking of how good you're getting at chess, I have an idea."

"What's that?" Garrett asked.

"I think it's time you play Beamer again."

"We have become quite the well-traveled set of pieces," King George remarked.

"All that talk about en passant makes me wonder if we might ever travel to France," mused Queen Beatrice.

Then all of the pieces began chatting among themselves.

"The Eiffel Tower...the Louvre...croissants...perhaps Garrett could play a game near the Arc de Triomphe...."

"How do you all know so much about France?" Piers asked Portia.

"Remember when we told you about the farmer's son who went off to college?"

Piers nodded.

"He studied for a semester in France," she told him. "It was called 'study abroad'. He sent postcards home. The farmer's wife used to bring the postcards down to the toolshed and read them aloud. And that's how we learned all about crepes."

"And macaroons," added Queen Beatrice.

"Bouillabaisse and coq au vin," Bishop Reginalt chimed in.

"Do you think we might actually ever go there?" Piers asked.

"You never know," King Edward replied.

"Oui," nodded Bishop Channing.

Chapter 29

SKYLAH ENTERED the library on Friday clutching her clipboard with her To-Do List attached. The first item was Beamer.

She wandered around the stacks in the library until she found him. He was seated on the floor in the 500s with a book called *Gems and Minerals* on his lap. His lips were moving, and the book was closed. Every once in a while he opened it and consulted a page before continuing.

"Hey Beamer," said Skylah.

Beamer held up one finger.

"Hang on one sec," he said. "I'm almost finished."

Skylah walked up and down the aisle. Ms. Kimberly had placed some titles on the top of the shelves, and Skylah opened one while she waited.

"Done!" he announced.

"What are you memorizing today?" she asked.

"Birthstones," he replied. "When's your birthday?"

"September."

"Sapphire," he announced.

"Listen Beamer, I'm here on official business."

He looked confused, so Skylah handed him a white envelope.

"This is for you."

"From who?" he asked.

"The Checkmates."

"The Checkmates? Who's that?"

"Garrett, Myles, and me. We're an organization representing and supporting Garrett on his journey as a chess player."

"Really? That's cool."

Beamer slid his thumb underneath the flap of the envelope and removed a formal invitation. His eyes darted from left to right as he read the details.

"So Garrett wants a rematch?"

"Yes, that's indicated right here," replied Skylah as she pointed to the top line. "Next Tuesday at recess, here in the library."

"Sure, okay," agreed Beamer.

Skylah smiled. "Excellent."

She turned to leave, but Beamer called her back.

"What does this mean?" he asked, pointing to the last line on the invitation. "Reception to follow?"

"Snacks," laughed Skylah. "Which reminds me, I have to talk to someone about that. See you on Tuesday!"

"Yup. See ya," Beamer replied. Then he picked up his book and went on to the next chapter.

It was dark and quiet inside the wooden box.

Piers didn't want to trouble anyone, but he had more questions than ever.

Why couldn't pawns move backwards?

Why were there more pawns than any other pieces?

Why did pawns capture other pieces diagonally?

Who invented all of these rules?

Would he ever know everything about himself?

Chapter 30

THE SECOND ITEM on Skylah's To-Do List: Food.

Skylah needed Ms. Kimberly's help with this, but she was in the middle of a conversation with a sixth grader named Skip about a lost book.

"Now Skip, keep looking for it," advised Ms. Kimberly. "Books do have a way of turning up. You might check under your bed, or in your closet, or even in the trunk of your parents' cars."

"I'll check," Skip promised.

"Okay, good." Then Ms. Kimberly turned her attention to Skylah. "How can I help you?"

Skylah peered over the lenses of her glasses, removed the pencil from behind her ear, and tapped her clipboard with it.

"It's about food," she began.

"Ah, food," murmured Ms. Kimberly. A dreamy look

came over her face. "641. Food and drink." Then she looked Skylah squarely in the eye. "Come, I will lead you to the books about food."

The next thing Skylah knew, she was following Ms. Kimberly as she wound her way through the tall stacks. She almost ran into her when she halted abruptly at the 600s.

Ms. Kimberly pointed.

"Now let's see what we have here," she said. "*All About Maple Syrup...Become the Best Baker...Twenty Ways to Grill a Steak....*"

"Actually, Ms. Kimberly, I wanted to ask you about having some food at an event in the library," Skylah broke in.

Ms. Kimberly gasped, and her eyes grew as large as saucers.

"Food?" repeated Ms. Kimberly. "You mean here? In. The. Library?" Her voice was barely a squeak now.

"Well, you see—" Skylah started to reply.

"Come with me, dear," Ms. Kimberly said, leading Skylah back toward the entrance. A small yellow notice was taped to the door, and Ms. Kimberly pointed to it.

Skylah read it aloud.

"No Food or Drink in the Library."

"See now, that's the rule!" Ms. Kimberly sort of sang out the word 'rule'.

"But—"

"The library is not a coffee shop. And let me tell you why. Years ago, students were allowed to eat their lunches in here. Do you know what happened? There were cookie crumbs everywhere. And pieces of chips all over the carpet. And then came the bugs. Ants mainly. Plus there's the problem of spilled drinks, which can be deadly for a book." Ms. Kimberly closed her eyes and placed her hand over her heart. "Just *deadly*."

"Ms. Kimberly?"

The librarian opened her eyes again.

"Yes, dear?"

"I would like to have a very small reception here next Tuesday," Skylah began. "You see, my friend Garrett has been learning how to play chess. He played against Beamer a few weeks ago, but he barely knew the game, so it didn't go very well. But he's been practicing quite a bit since then, and he's going to play against Beamer again. I'd like to make it into a special event." Skylah paused then, which gave Ms. Kimberly a chance to mull the idea over.

Her head tilted to the side as she did so.

"A reception? Well now, that's entirely different than messy bag lunches. Receptions *are* supposed to be fancy," she noted. Skylah got the idea that Ms. Kimberly *loved* fancy occasions.

"I was thinking a small snack and some juice boxes," Skylah went on.

Ms. Kimberly was silent for a long while.

Skylah waited patiently.

"How many students would be attending?" asked Ms. Kimberly.

"It would just be Garrett, Myles, Beamer and me," Skylah replied. "You're invited, too, of course."

Ms. Kimberly thought it over a little more.

"Well, I suppose if you confine the reception to *one table* and promise to clean up afterwards—"

"I'll provide the paper products and I'll be sure that everyone uses napkins," Skylah stated.

"Then I suppose I could allow it," Ms. Kimberly agreed.

"Thank you so much!"

"One more thing, though," added Ms. Kimberly. "You bring the juice boxes. But please allow me to provide the snack. After all, the library will be *hosting* the reception, so that's only proper. I will, in fact, bring some cheese balls."

"That sounds great!" Skylah said, smiling broadly, and soon 'Food' was crossed off her To-Do List.

Now there was only one other item to take care of.

All Piers could think about was the next game.

The next time he would be on the board.

And learning more about...himself.

Chapter 31

THE MATCH against Beamer was scheduled for Tuesday.

"I've got some more practice games lined up for you this weekend, too," Skylah said on the bus. "My babysitter plays chess, and she'll be over tomorrow. And then on Sunday—"

"I can't," interrupted Garrett. "We're going away for the weekend for my mom's cousin's wedding. We're leaving as soon as my dad gets home from work. We won't be back until Sunday night."

"But you need to practice! You play against Beamer next week!" Skylah reminded him.

Myles had been playing a game on his phone. He lifted his head up.

"You can practice on your phone. There's plenty of free chess apps," he said.

"That's a great idea," Garrett agreed. "I'll definitely ask

if my parents if I can download an app to practice with."

"There's something else we need to talk about," said Skylah to Myles across the aisle. She pointed to her list. "I'm arranging the reception."

"Reception?"

"The party after the chess game. Can you handle the decorations?"

Myles looked up from his phone.

"No problem," he replied. "And don't worry," he added. "They will be awesome."

The pieces were growing a little restless. It had been three days since Garrett had played a game.

"Do you think he's abandoned us?" asked Calvay Castle.

"It hasn't been that long," Bishop Reginalt replied. "I don't think there's cause for worry."

"I hope you're right," Stirling Castle told him. "Those were long years under the work bench."

"Boring years," Warwick Castle added.

"True," agreed Bishop Channing. "But Garrett is really enjoying the game, so I don't think he'll forget about us. And what's more, I have a feeling something big is on the horizon."

Chapter 32

NO ONE could believe their eyes. Myles had outdone himself.

There was an electronic screen near the library's entrance that usually advertised the lunch menu. But on Tuesday, "Chess Rematch Today: Beamer vs. Garrett" was scrolling by while animated chess pieces fought against each other on the Smart Board.

"This is amazing, Myles!" Skylah exclaimed. "When did you do all of this?"

"I created the animation on the weekend, and Ms. Kimberly helped me with the message yesterday," he replied. "But here's the best part—check this out...."

Myles grabbed a remote control from the circulation desk and pressed a button. Then they all heard a whirring sound, and a small drone rose into the air! Miles piloted it expertly over the bookshelves. Students sitting nearby lifted their noses out of their books and watched, mesmerized, as the drone flew to the table where Garrett and Beamer sat waiting to begin their game. It hovered for a moment, then deposited a small robot in the middle of the chess board. The robot spun around three times and then spoke!

"A RANDOM GENERATOR WILL NOW DETERMINE EACH PLAYER'S COLOR."

The robot's lights flashed from black to white repeatedly, then stopped.

"PLAYING WHITE, BEAMER. PLAYING BLACK, GARRETT. GOOD LUCK TO BOTH OF YOU."

"Dude," whispered Billy Everett, a seventh grader who had been in the process of placing a book into the dropbox. "That...was...*awesome*."

The entire library erupted into applause, and Ms. Kimberly didn't even think about shushing anyone.

"What in the world was that?" gasped Philbert.

Everyone waited for the kings to answer. The board was their kingdom, and some unknown oddity had descended onto it!

"I haven't any idea," King George said.

"Nor I," added King Edward. "But Bishop Channing was correct. Something big is definitely on the horizon."

"From whence did thou come?" King George asked.

The robot, which had spoken a moment earlier, remained silent.

"Why art thou here?" demanded King Edward.

"Speak and state thy purpose!" King George commanded.

Even more silence.

"I think the intruder is preparing to attack!" Sir Nicholas burst out. "Stand down, thou fearsome sphere!"

"Fear not, Your Majesties!" shouted Dame Mary. "We shall defend the realm!"

The four knights drew their swords and aimed them menacingly toward the intruder.

"BE GONE!!!" they shouted in unison.

Chapter 33

MYLES TOOK a bow when the applause finally died away. Then he guided the drone back above the chess board to retrieve the robot. After that it flew to the other side of the library and disappeared behind the paperbacks.

The match was about to begin.

"Well done, knights!" cried King Edward. "You hath scared off the accursed sphere! The kingdom is saved!"

"Huzzah!" whooped the other pieces. "Huzzah!"

Chapter 34

GARRETT LOOKED over and smiled at Skylah. She had done so much to get him to this point. He could never have improved his skills without all of the practice games. She really was a great manager. Then he turned and gave Myles a thumbs up. He must have spent all weekend working on the drone entrance and coding the robot. The Checkmates were the best friends he could ever ask for.

"Thank you," he mouthed silently to them.

Myles and Skylah beamed back and held up crossed fingers for good luck.

Garrett took a deep breath, then reached across and shook Beamer's hand.

Beamer opened by moving his pawn to e4.

The game was on.

Piers gasped.

He couldn't believe it.

Out of all the pieces on the board, Beamer had moved him first!

Chapter 35

GARRETT MOVED his pawn to d5 and immediately regretted it.

Beamer immediately captured it with his own pawn.

"Duh," Garrett muttered. *It must be my nerves*, he thought. He looked at the white pawn, sitting there all alone with no real protection.

Aha!

He moved his knight to f6. If Beamer didn't protect that pawn, he could capture it on his next move.

But to his surprise, Beamer did *not* protect the pawn. Instead he slid his bishop to b5. (*See diagram on next page.*)

"Check," said Beamer.

"I detest being in check," sighed King George.

Chapter 36

GARRETT LOOKED over the board for a few moments, then decided to move his pawn to c6.

"Out of check," he announced.

"Good move," smiled Beamer.

Prentice stood proudly, blocking the path to King George.

"It's an honor to defend you, Your Majesty," he stated.

But, alas, Prentice had spoken too soon.

On the next move, he was captured by Piers!

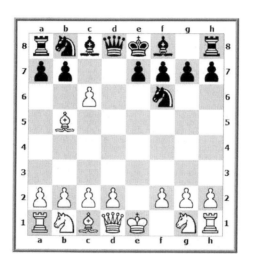

Chapter 37

GARRETT STUDIED the positions of Beamer's bishop and pawn, and considered capturing the pawn by moving his own pawn to c6.

In the end he slid his queen over to b6.

'Now I have a choice,' he thought. 'On my next move I can take Beamer's pawn or his bishop!'

Piers stood nervously next to Queen Beatrice.

It was only a matter of time before she would capture him.

But Beamer had to move first. What was he going to do?

Chapter 38

BEAMER STUDIED the board.

He thought for a long time.

Then he moved his pawn to b7 and captured Garrett's pawn. This put Garrett in check again, since there was no longer a pawn blocking Beamer's bishop.

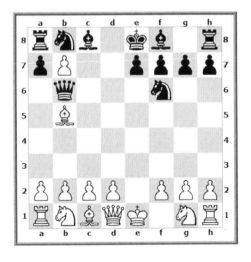

I can't believe he just did that, thought Garrett. *He's leaving his bishop totally unprotected!*

He moved his queen to b5 and captured the bishop. He realized that Beamer was probably going to capture his rook next...but there was no way he could prevent it!

He braced himself.

But instead of capturing the rook, Beamer moved his pawn to c8 and captured Garrett's bishop instead.

"Queen," stated Beamer.

"Queen?" asked Garrett. "What do you mean?"

"When you advance a pawn all the way to the other side, you can promote that pawn to any other piece—including a queen," said Beamer. "It's called pawn promotion."

That hadn't happened in any of the other games I played, thought Garrett.

"I don't have any extra queens in my set," he said.

"Not a problem," Beamer replied. "Ms. Kimberly, do you have a chess set?"

Ms. Kimberly did indeed have some extra chess sets in the library. She brought one over, and Beamer plucked a white queen out of the box. He exchanged his pawn with the queen.

Then Beamer said the word Garrett dreaded hearing the most.

"Checkmate."

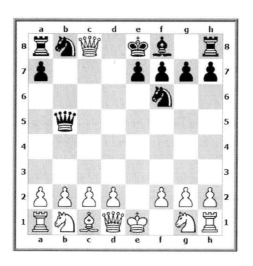

"Would somebody please explain what just happened?!" Piers demanded. He was very confused.

"It's simple," Prudence replied. "When one of us pawns moves all the way across the board without being captured, we get promoted."

"Promoted?" repeated Piers. "What does that mean?"

"It means," Prudence went on, "that you are exchanged for a queen, a rook, a knight, or a bishop. It's like getting superpowers."

"Really?!" Piers couldn't believe it. "So...I...became a..a...queen?"

"Yes, Piers. That's exactly what happened," replied Prudence.

"I just...I can't believe it," Piers said incredulously.

"It is always quite a surprise," Prudence told him. "Quite exciting and overwhelming."

"I'll say," said Piers.

Chapter 39

"THIS WAS a really great day," Garrett said. They were all sitting around a table eating cheese balls and drinking juice. Skylah had brought in plates and napkins that looked like a chess board. She had ordered them online. It was a very festive reception.

"Even though you didn't win?" asked Myles.

"Oh, I never expected to win," laughed Garrett. "I just like the game. And I'm learning more each time I play."

"I'm glad there's someone to play against," said Beamer. "And you *are* getting better."

"Well, I'm thrilled that the library hosted the event," smiled Ms. Kimberly. "You know, a few students came up to me after the game and expressed an interest in playing chess, too."

"Maybe the Checkmates should start a club," Garrett mused. "We could meet in here during recess once or twice a week."

"That sounds like a great idea," Myles agreed. He was already brainstorming ways to use the drone again.

"What do you think?" Garrett asked Skylah.

"I'm in!" she replied immediately.

"You'll help with the organizing? Like scheduling the meetings and stuff?"

"No, I mean I'm *in*. *In the club*. I've decided that I also want to learn to play chess," Skylah explained.

Everyone applauded that idea.

"But yes, I'll still help with the organizing," she smiled.

Everyone applauded again.

It was dark.

And quiet.

And still.

Piers was deep in thought, going over everything he'd learned in the past few weeks. Pawn chains...advancing one or two spaces on the first move...capturing diagonally...en passant...and pawn promotion....

He thought back to how Pop had been interrupted just when he was about to tell Garrett what the best thing about pawns was.

Piers thought about pawn promotion and how he became a queen. And how he could be promoted to other powerful pieces, too. That's probably what Pop was going to say. Becoming more powerful was so exciting!

But so was the rest of the game. The moves. The waiting. The suspense. The fact that every single game was different than the one before it.

"The best thing isn't just one thing," he whispered. "It's all of it."

Chapter 40

GARRETT COULDN'T believe how much Gram and Pop's place at Shady Acres still felt like the farm. The same old couch and chair were in their new living room. The same family pictures hung on the walls. They were eating dinner on the same flowered plates, and Gram's spaghetti tasted just as delicious as it always had.

"I miss the farm, but I like it here too," he stated.

"So do we," Pop agreed. "We're glad you're here for the weekend. After we do these dishes, we can walk down to the ice cream parlor. I think the flavor of the week is mint chocolate chip."

"I hope you brought your bathing suit," added Gram. "The pool opens tomorrow morning at nine o'clock. And then we can go bowling in the afternoon."

Garrett smiled. "That sounds great. I brought something for us to do tonight, if you want. After we get ice cream."

He walked over, unzipped his duffel bag and took out the wooden box.

"Isn't that the chess set you found at the farm?" asked Pop.

"Yup. And I've been learning how to play."

"Maybe you can teach me what you've learned."

"That's why I brought it."

Gram was nodding. "Mint chocolate chip ice cream and chess. Sounds perfect."

Garrett could not have agreed more.

It was going to be a great weekend.

Author's Note

ANYONE who plays chess can tell you who introduced them to the game. It takes a patient person to teach someone all of the rules. For me, this person was my father, who started teaching me in 1975. That was three years after Bobby Fischer of the United States won the World Chess Championship against Boris Spassky of the Soviet Union. During those years, my father had been swept up in the excitement of the match. He was a mechanic at Pan Am Airlines, and he played against mechanics during their lunch breaks at JFK Airport in New York City.

He started me on the Milton Bradley *Chess Tutor*, a set of eighty four instructional pages that slid under a plastic board. It proclaimed to help someone "Learn by yourself in 4 hours" by teaching you how the pieces move. As a seven-year-old kid, I spent a lot more than four hours poring over those pages and arranging those pieces. Eventually, my father and I began to play real games on a real board. He did not go easy on me because he preferred that I learn from my mistakes. He went on to teach my brother and sister as well.

I am still a very rudimentary player, but that does not detract from my love of the game and my respect for those who understand chess on the most intricate levels. As a school librarian, I've had the opportunity to introduce many students to the game during recess periods. Some of those students have gone on to beat me and have played in clubs and compete in tournaments. I am in awe of them and the way their brains can strategize many moves ahead.

A chess game is filled with beauty and stealth, wit and adventure, triumph and humility. I will be forever grateful that my father introduced me to it. I hope that if *you* know how to play chess, you will pass on your knowledge—as well as your love of the game—to someone else.

"The Pawn's Puzzlement"

It's no wonder that Piers was puzzled. Although pawns are the lowest ranking pieces on the chessboard, they have enjoyed a unique and storied history! When the game began in the sixth century in western India, it was called *chaturanga*, and the pieces represented two opposing armies. The

Sanskrit name for pawn was *padati* (from the word *pada*, meaning foot), probably because these small, nondescript pieces represented foot soldiers. They held the front line and protected the more powerful pieces, moving forward one step at a time while capturing diagonally.

In those times, if the *padati* were lucky enough to survive the battlefield and reach the other side of the side of the board, they would be promoted to *mantri*, which was the lowest ranking of the powerful pieces. (The *mantri* was the ancestor of the modern queen, a piece which, back then, moved diagonally one square at a time.) In the story you just read, Piers was lucky enough to be promoted to modern queen, which had much more power! However, this was not always the case with pawn promotion. Throughout history, some players did not support the idea of having two queens on the board. In the eighteenth and early nineteenth centuries, pawns could only be promoted to a piece that had already been lost. It wasn't common practice to promote a pawn to *any* piece until around the mid ninteenth century.

Garrett really thought Mr. Jay was cheating, but actually Mr. Jay had used the en passant move to capture Garrett's pawn. En passant (which translates to *in passing*) certainly seems odd, tricky and confusing for new players. Pawns are supposed to capture diagonally, correct? But the en passant rule allows the pawn to capture the pawn that's next to it and land on the square that was previously behind it. The en passant rule came about after the rules about pawns' opening moves changed from one square to two, as early as 1200 AD. With this change, some players were disgruntled that the two-square move could be used to bypass control of passing pawns. Not every region allowed the use of en passant, but by the end of nineteenth century en passant had become universally accepted. It is also important to remember that en passant can only be used after your opponent's pawn has moved two squares from its starting position, and en passant must be made *on the very next move*. Only opposing pawns can be captured en passant. Do not try to use en passant on another piece—that really would be cheating!

Although Piers and the others in the box were hand carved, they were still designed in the easily recognizable Staunton pattern, which was introduced in 1849 and is the international standard for world play. Piers would have looked quite different long ago. Not a lot of thought was given to the design of the pawns. The foot soldiers were commonly represented by pebbles, shells, small pieces of wood, and little cylinders. Even when pieces began to be carved with curves and knobs, the pawns remained very plain; sometimes nothing more than a tiny cone with a knob on top.

Pictured below are photographs that I took of pawns in a chess set from the twelfth century which was on display at The Met in New York City in 2022.

References

Bailey, S. & Allred, E. (2022, Jan. 24). *The Staunton Standard: Evolution of the Modern Chess Set.* World Chess Hall of Fame. https://worldchesshof.org/exhibit/staunton-standard-evolution-modern-chess-set

ChessKid. (2022, Jan. 24). *En passant.* ChessKid. https://www.chesskid.com/terms/en-passant-chess

Davidson, H. (1949). *A Short History of Chess.* Greenberg.

Kasparov, G. (2004). *Checkmate! My First Chess Book.* Gloucester Publishers.

McCrary, John. (2021, June 3). *The Evolution of Modern Chess Rules: En passant.* US Chess Federation. https://new.uschess.org/news/evolution-modern-chess-rules-en-passant

Murray, H. (1913). *A History of Chess.* Oxford University Press.

Pfeiffer Fund. (1971). Chess set [Stonepaste; molded and glazed]. The Metropolitan Museum of Art, New York,

NY, United States.

https://www.metmuseum.org/art/collection/search/4522
04

About the Author

VALERIE MUNRO is an elementary school librarian and the author of *Down the Swale*, *Journey to Nagwanis*, and *Up the Falls*. She has also been a contributing author of the New Jersey Center for the Book's ongoing e-book series, the Jersey Trackers. She lives in Sparta, New Jersey with her husband, and they have two grown children.

Made in the USA
Middletown, DE
07 February 2023

23717171R00102